CARTOONIA

Scarlett Harrington

Cartoonia series title. Scarlett Harrington Press

Published by: Scarlett Harrington

Copyright © 2020 by Scarlett Harrington

ISBN 978-1-8382951-0-3

TABLE OF CONTENTS

PROLOGUE

The night was dark and frosty. Rachel could feel her fingers and toes freezing as she ran through the woods of Stone Edge. She wished she could stop running, though. But if she did, she was probably going to rethink staying back in Cartoonia after she had just betrayed everyone to leave, alone.

The book in her hand felt heavier with every second that she spent to get to her destination – the entry port. It was what they all called the first place Areeyah had brought them to after they were stolen from their world. Over time, Rachel had learned that the entry port could also be the exit port if they had everything that they needed to leave.

To leave Cartoonia wasn't a one-way ticket. She would know that since she was the anchor – the human who had dared to open Areeyah in the first place. The knowledge of the cartoon world was only bestowed to her. And for weeks, it had come in bits and pieces that she had to figure out whilst discussing them with Ron, Jer and Rebecca.

Thinking about her friends almost put a string in her step. Rachel clenched her teeth and kept running. They had betrayed her. Ron, Jer and Rebecca – all three of them. They didn't deserve her sympathy. She had helped everyone navigate through the ruthless magical world of Cartoonia, hoping they could go through the necessary stages of sex and more sex before returning home. And what she had gotten back were disloyalty, lies and heartbreak that were slowly destroying her.

She finally paused once she noticed that she was close to her destination. It was a large building in the middle of the Stone Edge woods; a cartoon replica of the history museum back in their world. Three months ago, the museum was just another astonishing edifice in New York. But now, it was standing like a monstrous dark tower on Stone Edge – the entry and exit port for the four humans that had been stolen into an alternate universe.

Inhaling and exhaling to calm her racing heart, Rachel straightened her back and began to step towards the building. She clutched Areeyah to her chest, hoping that the book wouldn't abandon her now that she needed it the most. A week ago, searching with Ron, Jer and Rebecca, they had found Areeyah in its resting place in Krix and had taken it to Daffodils – where they had called home for the past three months. Two hours ago, however, Rachel had stolen Areeyah from its resting place in Daffodils, swearing to leave and never return.

As soon as she got close to the entrance of the museum, its door swept wide open as if it was expecting her. Rachel closed her eyes briefly as a fierce wind blew over her as well. Through the door, she could only see darkness. No hallways. No doorways or staircases to the museum galleries. Just pitch darkness. The trees around her suddenly began to sway sideways as the wind around her grew fiercer and colder.

"Well, here goes everything," Rachel gritted her teeth and stepped into the darkness.

Nothing? Nothing happened for a second. Then, light gradually enveloped her, and the museum door clasped shut with a loud thud. Rachel clutched Areeyah tighter to her chest, waiting. She knew Cartoonia wouldn't just let her leave without getting more. It had taken everything from each of them, but it would always want more. The light around her got brighter, hurting her eyes, and she clasped them shut and held her breath.

Eventually, she heard movements around her. Reluctant to open her eyes to the expected, she heaved a sigh and continued to wait. Areeyah suddenly felt warm and lightweight in her hands. She could feel it throbbing slowly, almost like a heart getting pumped with blood. It had come alive to give her what she wanted. But first, she must fuel Cartoonia with her lust.

She opened her eyes eventually to find four buff men standing akimbo in a row in front of her. The inside of the museum had become a vast space filled with only light and naked men. Each man had glossy mocha skin and muscles rippled on their arms, chests and thighs. Their nakedness wasn't new to her, but once her vision rested at their groins, Rachel felt a lump in her throat. Each man had a cock the size of her fist. And in every man's eyes, she could see the eagerness to fill her insides with so much pleasure, she could fall apart from it.

Still waiting, she watched as the first man on the row approached her. He didn't say a word. Instead, his eyes took her entire body in before they stopped at the book clutched to her chest. She decided she was going to call him Alpha. He was taller and more muscular than the rest, with piercing brown eyes and a bald head. He obviously was the one the rest of the men answered to.

"Can I have that until we are done here?" Alpha whispered after stopping in front of her.

Rachel nodded. Areeyah was hers to do as she willed now. She knew that the moment she stepped into the light in the museum. What was going to happen now; it was to create a gateway back to her world. Once Alpha pulled the book from her arms, objects began to form around her. First was a table for Alpha to place Areeyah on. Then, next were walls and windows that reflect the cold night outside. Rachel turned around to see rugs, tables and chairs appearing from empty spaces around her. Everything stopped when a large king-sized bed slowly emerged behind her. Alpha ambled towards her back and with a broad smile on his face, asked, "Are you ready Rachel Paris?"

Rachel let her eyes fall to his cock and swallowed hard. Behind him, his pack waited impatiently to do his bidding.

It was a small price to pay, considering what she was about to do. Summoning a broad smile of her own, she let her hands fall to her side, showing total submission, and nodded.

"Yes, I am ready."

CHAPTER ONE

A powerful, irresistible force controlled the lustful thirst that Jamie felt. Beads of sweat gathered beneath his clothes, and he could feel his cock rising to its full strength. As he whirled Peyton around and plastered her face and chest against the wall, he felt a wild beast growing inside of him. The beast wanted Peyton totally submissive and yearning for sweet, unfettered lust. It wanted him to cruelly make love to her and find fulfilment by hearing her cry for release.

Peyton seemed to know what she had to do to feed his beast. She raised both her hands to the wall and arched her back for him. Then, slowly, she widened her hips and bent lower, opening up her ass and pussy lips. He felt more sweat drizzling down his body. His cock jolted harder in his pants, desiring freedom from the cage of his tight jeans.

"Oh, Peyton."

Resisting the beast was impossible. Jamie plastered his groin against her right ass cheek, gripped her neck and smacked her left ass cheek with his palm. Peyton's body jolted against his body immediately. She let out a gasp and bit her lips as he stared intently into her eyes and smacked her again. "You like that, don't you?" he smacked her a third time. "You don't mind a little bit of smacking before—"

"Yes!" Payton replied before he could finish. She rubbed her cheek against the wall, gasped as he smacked her again, and stared over her shoulder at him. "I don't mind, Jamie. I don't mind whatever you do to me."

Seeing her so lustful and submissive fuelled the already swollen desires inside of him. Jamie nodded and slowly went back to smacking her ass. This time, he let go of her neck and smacked each cheek of her ass with his hands. With each smack, Peyton let out more gasps and began to bend her back lower until she was almost touching her toes. He had never seen anyone as flexible as she became each second, he tortured her ass. Awed, he fixed himself behind her and lowered his hand to the crack of her ass. Tracing in between her ass, he reached downward for her pussy lips and began to tap the edges with the full of his palm. At the same time, he dipped his other hand into his jeans and freed his cock.

"Yeah," Peyton urged him on, obviously aroused by his palm tapping over her throbbing hole. She twerked her ass around his palm, getting her clit to rub against his fingers.

He smiled at the thought of finally filling her squirming pussy hole with his rigid cock. But not yet. Despite the urgency of their situation – the fierce storm rocking against their sailboat – he wanted to take his time to awaken deep lust within Peyton. He wanted to search every inch of her body with his hands, lips and teeth, learning what tickled her and what didn't.

Deciding to search her dripping went cunt first, he bent behind her, gripped her ass and buried his lips in between her spread-eagled thighs. Peyton's body shook with renewed lust. She let out a sigh and reached behind her to grip his head. He traced the length of her pussy lips first before dipping his tongue into her pleasure hole. Clasping her clit into his mouth, he suckled gently, getting her more aroused and then continued to dip his fingers inside her.

"Oh, Jamie. Oh. Ohhhhh!"

Hearing Peyton pine with pleasure for him wasn't something he had ever dreamt before. And he wondered why. They hadn't spoken or seen in many years, but she had always been his first female friend, his first crush – everything. He had loved her but had never considered firmly ramming any part of himself inside her as she cried out with pleasure.

This was happening now, and every fibre within him woke with pleasure. He could feel his balls clenching while his cock jolted harder out of his jeans. The uncontrollable pleasure wasn't just happening to him. A few feet away, Kyle laid on his back with his teeth biting into his lips. Lily feasted on his cock like Popsicle. Holding and squeezing his balls in her palms, she spat, nibbled, bit and swallowed his cock down to her throat. Watching Kyle losing control and then pulling up Lily by her hair, drove Jamie to the peak. He pulled his lips from Peyton's cunt and began to drill her clit with only his fingers – this time, faster and harder.

"Oh, please, Jamie. Please, don't—Oh, oh! Stop! Don't—please, please."

Peyton obviously was torn between asking for his cock and urging him to continually plunge his fingers inside her. He fingered her to his fill before he returned to his feet, pulled down his pants and reached forward to hold her waist. He gripped one of her breasts with his other hand and closed his eyes, and a wave of pleasure swept through them.

"Now, please," Peyton pleaded. "Fucckk meeee!"

Her last words slid out of her throat with a long moan as he buried his cock deep inside her. Instantly, the boat echoed with louder moans and sighs as Kyle also lifted Lily above him and sat her down on his cock. While Lily rode him like a horse, Jamie plunged himself inside Peyton over and over again. He closed his eyes, feeling electrifying explosions inside of him.

Getting close to his climax a minute later, he held on tight to Peyton and yelled out the word, "Cumming!"

"Fuckkk! Me, too!" Peyton returned, gripping his thighs and meeting his heavy thrusts with hers. Their bodies collided several times before stumbling to the floor. Jamie fell to his hands and knees as he thrust his last. As for Peyton, she coiled beneath him, gritting her teeth as her pleasure reached its climax.

The sailboat fell silent for a minute, Jamie finding it hard to do anything but stare down at Peyton's beautiful face. Peyton kept her eyes close with her chest slowly rising and falling. By the time she opened them, she smiled warmly at Jamie and reached up to plant a kiss on his lips. "Did it work?" she whispered, looking warily around them.

"Work?" Jamie frowned, too overwhelmed by her beauty to understand what she meant.

"Yes, it seems the boat started sailing smoothly," Peyton slowly withdrew from beneath him.

"It did," Lily's voice whisked between them. She was slowly rising to her feet with Kyle and was putting on her clothes. "And I think we are heading to a small island called Daffodils."

"Daffodils?" Jamie cleared his throat and began to pull on his clothes as well.

"Yes," Lily said. "Someone—a woman is waiting to receive us."

CHAPTER TWO

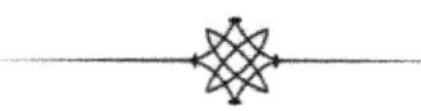

Jeremy Richmond stood quietly at the beach, staring at the ocean as the storm slowly rescinded. Minutes earlier, thick clouds had gathered above them, rendering their little island dark and gloomy. He had stared at those clouds indifferently, aware of the powerful forces that always reeled through Cartoonia, changing the weather, moving islands and forests, and creating the need for irresistible lust.

Lust. Left to him, it was everything that ever happened in the alternate universe he had found himself twenty years ago. Ron and Rebecca seemed to have stopped counting the days, but he never did. He couldn't. He had nightmares of how it had all begun now and every day, he wished he could leave the confines of Daffodils and make it stop…make the regrets and the pain of leaving his home stop.

The word, home, meant differently to him twenty years ago. He was only eighteen when he had packed his clothes, hopped into his step father's car, and had driven into the sunset. He had had enough of watching his mother get abused by a man she didn't love but only married because…well, her son needed a man who could cater for him. Putting himself out of the picture meant that she could finally leave and maybe have a life of her own. Jer had driven as far away as possible and had abandoned the car for a train to New York.

New York wasn't any different from the life he had left behind for a while. He had no one, no shelter and no cash. For days, he could remember sleeping in alleys whilst searching for a job. He cleaned bathrooms, dressed in funny outfits for restaurants and ran errands just to survive. There was finally a glint of hope when he got a job as a janitor at the history museum. The museum gave bunks to workers who didn't have homes and also offered flexible working hours, so he could take up more jobs and save up money.

His life had a perfect balance afterwards, and he thought about returning home one day just to see if his mother had done what he had expected.

Well, the day for him to return never came. One night, he had stepped into the wrong gallery in the museum, and a bright light had wholly swallowed him. He had found himself in Cartoonia with three other people like him, and everything had changed. *Everything.*

"There! You see it, don't you?"

Jer jolted out of his thoughts to frown at the ocean. Rebecca had been adamant for the past hour that something was coming – or someone. He wanted to believe that, too. But they hadn't seen a single outsider in Cartoonia since Rachel left. Rachel had closed the entry and exit ports forever. She had picked up Areeyah and had never looked back.

"I don't see anything," Ron gritted his teeth, trying to see through the now-clearing storm.

Jer stepped forward, doing the same. He winced, trying to find what Rebecca had seen. All he could see were the waves, climbing up and slapping against the shores.

"A boat," Rebecca insisted. "By the horizon in the left. It's sailing slowly as if the water is bringing it to us."

"Rebecca, there is nothing there…"

"I see it!" Jer suddenly whispered. He had thought it was just another wave riding to the shore at first. But as he stepped forward, standing beside Rebecca, he could see it just where she had pointed to. "A sailboat." he corrected. "It looks…it looks just like The Anchor."

"The anchor? Same one Rachel left in?" Ron joined them.

"Yes," Jer replied frowning. He glanced at Rebecca, who was now biting on her nails, lost in thought. "You don't think it is Rachel who's come back, do you?"

"So many years," Rebecca whispered under her breath. "So many years and she would come back for us—?"

"She could—"

"It isn't her," Rebecca whispered before Ron could interject her. "It isn't."

Jer let his gaze return to the sailboat as it calmly sailed to the shore. He prepared himself for what was come. Whatever it was, he had only one plan in his head. Get Areeyah, take the boat, and return home.

And he was going to do that with or without Rebecca and Ron.

Fully dressed, Lily stepped back against the wall and closed her eyes. The sailboat now glided calmly on the ocean, getting them closer to their destination. She wished she didn't have to worry about the dangers left for them to face as they found their way back home, but she did. She didn't know what each one would be yet, but she could sense it. She felt as if the implosion at Stone Edge was just Cartoonia's way of showing her what it was capable of. It wouldn't be disobeyed, and they would all be wise to learn that.

She smoothed her palm over her jeans and opened her eyes to find Kyle stepping towards her with an apple wrapped in a foil. "Here, you should eat," he said.

She took the apple from him, smiling. "Thank you." As she unwrapped the foil, she noticed Peyton offering loaves of bread to Jamie as well. Jamie smiled and bent to kiss her wholly on the lips. Lily felt a tinge of jealousy in her heart.

"You know, you should let him know you like him," Kyle cleared his throat beside her.

She threw him a sharp glance. "I am sorry?"

Kyle nodded towards Jamie and Peyton. "Jamie likes Peyton, obviously. And it isn't because of this place. He has always liked her. You should have seen his face when Peyton called him – uhm, that would be yesterday, wouldn't it? It's an alternate universe, but it is still the same hours every day, isn't it?"

Lily could hear Kyle's questions, but her gaze had returned to Jamie and Peyton. Peyton had leaned closer to Jamie, watching adoringly as he tasted the food and closed his eyes in pleasure. It hurt just to watch them together. "I don't like Jamie," she grunted, returning to Kyle.

Kyle said nothing for a second. He only nodded and then went back to his questions. "The days aren't different here, are they? Would an hour here be the same back home?"

Lily thought about that for a while. "I don't know," she whispered. "It could. Or maybe not. I don't understand everything yet."

"Yes, and no one would expect you to. Just keep trying everything you can to get us back home."

Lily nodded and instinctively stared into his eyes. They darted back at her, and she wondered why she couldn't just feel the same excitement that coursed through her body whenever she stared into Jamie's eyes. She felt unbridled lust always with Kyle – the kind that had gotten her to take off her top and offer herself to him earlier – but it was different with Jamie. Jamie was like a magnet that continued to pull her in, up until the moment she wouldn't be able to resist its powerful force anymore.

"I will," she whispered eventually, lowering her gaze. "And thank you, Kyle."

Kyle quickly placed his palm beneath her chin and held her face back up. "You are welcome," he whispered and kept mum for another second. "I said something earlier, Lily," he finished, "and I meant every word."

She remembered, but what he had said wasn't something she had wanted to think about. The memory was still fresh in her head, alongside how he had sat her on his cock and had writhed with pleasure as she rode him to their climax. "You don't have to say anything about it," he continued. "You don't have to say anything about liking Jamie either. I just want to be sure you understand what I want."

"Me," she whispered, letting her eyes get lost in his. "You want me."

"Yes, I do," he nodded, slowly closing the distance between them. His lips clasped against hers before she could think and she felt a jolt burn down her throat, making her thirsty. She swallowed hard as he nibbled on her upper lip and then parted both lips with his tongue. His tongue entangled hers briefly before he pulled away. She held her breath, feeling a riveting spark between them. Whatever she could have for Jamie, Kyle had just proved it was there between them too. He said nothing after the kiss. He only stepped aside as Jamie strolled towards them, chewing. Lily quickly munched on the apple Kyle had given to her.

"I think we should get to the deck," Jamie suggested. "See whoever or whatever is waiting to receive us."

"Good idea," Kyle agreed, pausing to listen to the water around them. "And I think we might be closer to the shore already."

"Yeah. Lily?" Jamie whispered.

Everyone turned to look at her, including Peyton.

Lily cleared her throat, suddenly anxious. "Yes, we should," she whispered. *And I may just be frantic, but I think we should be careful with everyone out there, too.*

"Alright. Let's go then," Jamie made his way up the stairs and pushed the door open. He paused when he noticed no one had moved. "Is everyone coming or not?"

"Sure," Peyton trotted after him.

Kyle waited until both of them were out of the room before he climbed the stairs and held out his hand to her. "Come, Lily, we are almost home," he whispered.

Lily let go of all the doubt and fear that troubled her and took his hand. *Home.* She wasn't even sure she had one back in their world.

CHAPTER THREE

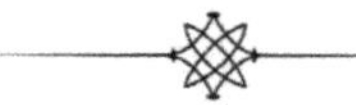

Rebecca watched intently as the sailboat slowly moved with the calm waves towards the shore. She could count two people on the boat already. Then, three. And then, four. They looked like teenagers; the oldest should probably be eighteen or nineteen. As the boat finally hit the sands and stopped, Rebecca heaved a sigh and began to make her way towards the visitors.

"Do you know what to tell them?" Ron asked, strolling quietly behind her. Jer didn't bother to move from his position.

"Everything," Rebecca whispered, more to herself than to him. "I am going to tell them everything, and then we go home."

The visitors remained on the sailboat with their shoulders to one another. Their eyes followed her cautiously, and Rebecca wore a smile on her face as the memory of her first time on Daffodils flashed through her mind.

She had been on the same boat, too. The name, Anchor, had resonated with her then. It reminded her of the days she had gone sailing with her family during summer and spring breaks as a child. In one of those fond memories, her father had stood beside her, watching the sunset with her. "There, Dad," she had pointed to a ship in the distance. "Is that a warship?"

"No," her father had chuckled. "That's a cargo ship, dear."

"It looks—it looks so big," she had commended.

"Yeah, it has to be if it wants to carry all the cargo on top of it."

"Is that why water doesn't take it from shore then?" she had asked curiously. "Like it does with little boats that aren't tied down. Because it is too big?"

"No, no," her father had chuckled again. He inched towards her and ruffled her curly brown hair. "It's the anchor," he said. "Every ship has got one that looks like a, uhm, hook. When at the shore, the sailors drop the heavy hook that keeps the floating ship in place."

She didn't fully understand what the anchor was then, but she nodded and stared back at the ship in the distance. For a while, she just stood with her father, staring endlessly at the sunset and the beautiful sea. The memory of that day stayed with her. When her father passed away, she seldom went back to it to keep herself from breaking down over his death.

When she got to Cartoonia and saw the sailboat, it felt like a sign – a sign that no matter what, she was strong and would find her way back home. Everything they went through suggested that Cartoonia wanted them exactly where they were, but she wouldn't give up. With Rachel, Ron and Jer's help, Areeyah was found. They wanted to spend their last night on Daffodils together and head to Stone Edge the next day, but that never happened. Rachel left alone. The heartless bitch stole their exit and left them in Cartoonia to rot.

Rebecca swept the memories out of her head as soon as she stopped in front of the boat and looked up into blue, green and deep brown eyes. There was one that was more piercing than the rest – the green eyes. She stared at the handsome young man, noticing the smooth beards on his face, alongside his broad chest and muscular arms. Something sparked inside of her – a feeling all too familiar, considering how long she had been in Cartoonia. She let it go with a smile and nodded at the group. "Welcome," she greeted. "I assume the trip was pleasurable for everyone."

She had expected the colours that rose on the girls' cheeks. The redhead amongst them stepped forward and stared at Ron and Jer. "What is this place?" she asked. "And who are you, people?"

"Good questions," Rebecca grinned. She spread her arms, showing them the lush meadow behind her. "This is Daffodils, one of the few islands you would come across in Cartoonia. It is the only place that wouldn't throw you out."

"Throw you out?"

He speaks, Rebecca thought, turning to the bearded young man she had noticed earlier. "Every place in Cartoonia has a specific accommodation time," she explained. "Take Stone Edge for instance. It threw you out, didn't it?"

"How—how did you…"

"It did the same with us the first day we found ourselves in this universe," she said before he could finish. "I, Ron and Jer."

The eyes on the deck swept to Ron and Jer instantly. Ron bit his lips while Jer nodded from where he stood.

"So, you—you are all from the outside world?" the bearded young man asked again. Instead of an explanation, Rebecca only nodded her head. She inched forward and gave each of them a warm smile. "I am Rebecca," she whispered. "I can help with all the answers you need, but it doesn't have to be with me standing at the shore and with all four of you reluctant to step off the sailboat. Daffodils are perfectly safe."

All four of them stared quietly at each other. Then, the second girl – a brunette – nodded as if her decisions were firmly what the rest followed. Rebecca frowned. She had seen that before. The girl was as important to their survival as Rachel was twenty years ago.

"Okay," the bearded young man leaned towards the railing of the boat and nodded at her. "My name is Jamie."

"Peyton," the redhead introduced herself.

"Kyle."

A moment passed, and the brunette stepped forward, too. "Lily," she whispered, her eyes boring into hers.

For a second, Rebecca felt a connection between them, almost as if they had met before.

"So, how long have you been here – in Cartoonia?" Jamie asked, stepping off the sailboat and approaching her

"Let's keep the questions for when you are all settled in," Rebecca swiftly whirled around and nodded at Ron, who stepped aside and pointed to the path to the meadow.

"On Daffodils, there is comfort for everyone," she explained, watching over her shoulder as the rest of the group stepped off the boat after Jamie. "You could have a clean bath, change into fresh clothes and eat more than just fruits and bread."

"A bath and fresh clothes? You have got me," the redhead whispered under her breath and walked ahead of the rest. The other male who had introduced himself as Kyle trotted after her, excited as well. Ron began to walk ahead of them, leading them to the Daffodil Manor – their home for the past twenty years.

It took a while before Rebecca noticed that Jamie and Lily were still reluctant to leave shore. She turned to them and waited.

Slowly, Lily clutched Jamie's hand and stared into his eyes, possibly to draw strength. Rebecca watched both of them patiently. Eventually, Jamie ambled forward, heading for the meadow and taking Lily with him.

Rebecca waited until they were far from earshot before she stepped towards Jer. "Search the boat," she instructed. "All four of them do not seem to have Areeyah on them. Find it and bring it to me."

With a forced smile on her face, she trotted after Jamie and Lily, hoping that the past wouldn't repeat itself.

Earlier, while she watched Lily staring into Jamie's eyes, she had sensed a familiar sensual, magical force wrap around them.

It was the same dark force that had always driven Ron back to her when he should have been with Rachel.

CHAPTER FOUR

Jamie padded beside Lily as they were led to the meadow. Earlier, when she slowly tucked her fingers into his, he had felt a little spark between them. He had glanced sideways into her eyes and had seen fear and a little bit of desire. Before they left Stone Edge, Lily had avoided his gaze. He had suspected something was wrong but had shrugged it off eventually. Now, walking beside her with her hands in his, he felt there was something Lily wasn't talking about. It wasn't just about Cartoonia. It had to do with him.

"Don't be ridiculous, Jamie. She is probably just as scared as Peyton and doesn't want anyone to know she is."

"Yeah, there is that. But why is she holding your hand, instead of Kyle's since they are supposed to be together?"

Jamie shook his head as the voices in his head disagreed with one another. He glanced at Lily again, noticing her long, curly brown hair and her full, pink lips. He had never stopped to admire how beautiful she looked, especially with her slender shoulders and thin waist. Unlike Peyton, Lily had average-sized breasts that looked like fully-grown peaches in her crop top. He wondered how fulfilled Kyle had felt when he had held each one in his hand or had even buried himself in between Lily's straight, long legs.

"So, we are imagining sex with her now?"

Jamie closed his eyes and paused. He didn't want to think of such things, but holding Lily suddenly drove him down that road.

"Is everything okay, Jamie?"

Jamie opened his eyes and noticed that Lily had stopped walking, too. They were surrounded by beautiful bright yellow flowers and trumpet-shaped plants. "Nothing, just thinking," he cleared his throat.

Lily tightened her grip and continued to walk with him. "Something you want to talk about?"

"Uh?"

"What you were thinking about; do you want to talk about it?"

"Uhm," Jamie cleared his throat again. "Just about everything."

"Everything?"

"Yes, everything. Turning into avatars of ourselves, finding a sailboat, witnessing an implosion and almost tumbling into the ocean."

A smile appeared over Lily's face. "Not bad, is it?"

Yeah, if only I wasn't thinking about your breasts earlier, too. "Yeah, we are here, right?"

Lily glanced around them and then stared at Kyle and Peyton, who was now heading atop a hill after Ron. "Where is here exactly?" she said in a low tone.

"Daffodils; you heard Rebecca call it that earlier."

"No, I mean, why are we here. What do we do next?"

"I thought that was something you ought to know?"

"I just—well, I just don't know anything anymore since we got to the shore."

"You don't always know everything at once before, do you? Perhaps we are just here to rest awhile and then get all the information we need to find our way out."

"Perhaps," Lily replied and kept quiet.

"Lily," Jamie whispered. "You don't think something is wrong, do you?"

"I don't know," Lily shrugged. "I --"

"Jamie!"

Lily jerked her hand away as Peyton whirled around and waved her hands excitedly in the air to get his attention. "Come here, Jamie. It is stunning," she called.

"Coming," Jamie responded, noticing that Lily had looked away and was avoiding his eyes again. "We should talk about why we are here once we are fully rested, Lily," he whispered. "I am sure Rebecca would have answers to our questions, too."

Lily nodded and slowly stepped aside so he could head towards Peyton. Jamie shook his head and strolled quietly to join Peyton, who still looked elated about what she had seen.

Jamie saw it too as soon as he got to the top of the hill. A quarter of a mile away, sitting prettily like two mountain holding hands, were two beautiful mansions made of marble and oakwood. The mansions were surrounded by daffodils – lots of them – and a stream ran in between them like a beautiful partition.

"It is beautiful, isn't it?" Peyton hopped and held his arm.

Jamie nodded and stared down at their interlocked arms. Swiftly, the inexplicable spark from holding Lily's hand slid into his thoughts, and he glanced over his shoulder to look at Lily one last time. She was beautiful in a crop top, jeans and boots, no doubt. And if he wasn't careful, he was going to find himself besotted by her angelic looks.

"The mansions wait," Ron luckily announced, getting his thoughts back to Peyton as she fastened her arm to his and took him down the hill to the mansions.

Jer hurriedly searched inside the sailboat, indifferent about the fruits and wine bottles at first. Once he couldn't find what he was looking for, he stood in the middle of the room, stared at the familiar roof and heaved a sigh. Sitting down and resting his back on the nearest wall, he picked up one of the bottles, unscrewed it with his teeth and downed a few gulps.

The strong taste of the alcohol got him to grit his teeth and close his eyes with pleasure. More memories of the past swept through his mind. This time, they were about the days he had spent in Cartoonia – days before Rachel had left with the only exit port in the entire alternate universe.

Rachel. Just like Rebecca and Ron, he had known nothing about her before Areeyah had stolen all four of them from the world they once knew. He didn't care to know anything either when they had arrived in Stone Edge. Everything that mattered to him was Rebecca. As if his body was made to obey hers, he craved her touch, the feel of her soft skin against his and how it felt to be deep inside her warm cunt. He spent days and nights, just watching her breasts and ass jiggle in her dress, his mind reeling with images of making love with her.

He had gotten so immersed in his lust for her, he hadn't stopped to notice that Rebecca could be in love with someone else. She let him touch her whenever he wanted to. She opened her legs wide and cried with pleasure whenever he made love to her. Yet, there was the only room in her heart to dote over Ron – Rachel's chosen. Apparently, Rebecca had always been in love with Ron before Cartoonia decided to twist their fates.

Jer opened his eyes, opting out of the incidents that followed Rebecca's unwavering feelings for Ron. He had found out at first and had tried to live with it. Rachel had chosen differently. She had simply left the pain behind and had returned home.

Jer took a last gulp from the bottle and finally pushed himself up to his feet. He stared around the sailboat one last time and was about to climb the stairs to the deck when he noticed it – a small box, tucked away in a dark corner with rumpled foils. Taking a step back, he bent and stared at it.

Maybe the sailboat had brought them something more valuable than Areeyah after all.

And he had no plans to share any of that with Rebecca or Ron.

CHAPTER FIVE

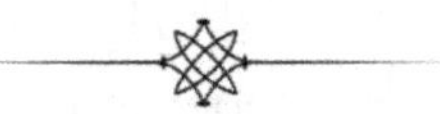

It took over an hour before Jamie saw Kyle, Peyton and Lily again. Ron had led them into one of the mansions and had shown them into separate rooms. With a nod, he had opened the door into the last room and had told Jamie, "Have a bath, rest. Rebecca would see to getting lunch ready. She would answer all the questions you have then."

Jamie had nodded back before stepping into the room. He stared around the fully-furnished room, impressed by the elegant furniture. There was a neatly-tucked queen-sized bed, a floor with a Persian rug, and a chair and table made from very polished wood Jamie wasn't sure he knew. A fireplace in the corner gleaned from the rays of sunlight coming through the windows. There was also a large wardrobe with large mirrors on its doors. It felt as if he had suddenly stepped into paradise. Stone Edge was beautiful, too, but Daffodils had a feel of a wealthy island to it.

After admiring the room, Jamie had glanced over his shoulder to realize Ron had closed the door and had left him alone. He slowly stepped towards the bed and sat. Refraining from thinking about Lily or Peyton, he thought about his mother and father instead. It had been almost twenty-four hours now since he had been transported into Cartoonia. The dorm would be the first to notice his absence. If they searched his room and find Kyle gone as well, this would have roused the suspicion that something had happened to them at the bonfire. Of course, they wouldn't want to inform their parents yet until they were sure. But Jamie knew his mother would already be perturbed at the moment. She would have tried so many times to reach him through his phone and would only get the beep and his phoney voicemail recording.

Heaving a sigh and preferring not to think of what was probably happening outside of Cartoonia, Jamie went back to the door and slid the lock in place. He found the bathroom a minute later and slid out of his clothes. The plan was to wash quickly and find Peyton, Lily and Kyle, so they could talk about what their next step should be. But as soon as he had stepped beneath the shower and the cold water had trickled over his body, the plan had changed. Jamie stayed put beneath the water. He closed his eyes and felt relief pouring over every inch of him as the water splashed over his head, shoulders and back. Everything that had happened before they got to Daffodils suddenly didn't matter. He felt as if they were finally home – where answers to everything was waiting for them. For another ten minutes, he had just let the water clean the dirt and sweat off of him. It almost felt as if all the doubts and fears inside of him were being washed out as well.

When he stepped back into the room, he headed for the large wardrobe on the wall. Staring at the reflection of his impeccable naked body in the mirror, he wondered if everything was real – the broad chest, his muscular arms and his dick, which seemed bigger than it naturally was outside of Cartoonia. Perhaps it was all just a dream, he thought. Maybe something had happened to all of them in the cottage, and he was in an alternative universe in his head – the result of loving his life too much, he wouldn't just give in to death.

The theory sounded so stupid in his head, he waved it off and opened the doors of the wardrobe. He didn't know what he expected to see, but pairs of clean jeans and well-ironed shirts and jackets stared back at him. There were socks, hats, boots and underwear, too. He selected randomly from everything and began to get dressed. Three minutes later, he was draped in new jeans, boots and a shirt that glued around his firm body. Ron knocked on the door almost immediately as if he had calculated all the time Jamie needed to himself before he was ready to step out.

"Everyone is ready," he said when Jamie opened the door. "And Rebecca is waiting for you," he continued, stepping out of the way and waving his arm down the hallway.

Jamie stepped out of the room and walked beside him without a word. He let his eyes take in the walls around him – the paintings on the wall, doors leading to other rooms, and the red woollen rugs beneath them. Bright light flooded the hallway from the windows at both ends. Ron turned left as they got to the end of the hallway and pushed a large door open.

"Hey, Jamie, you are here," Peyton appeared and quickly wrapped her arms around him. She smelled like clean soap. Jamie hugged her back and then inched back to smile at her. "You changed into a gown," he noted.

Peyton whirled around, so he could see how the gown fit perfectly on her lush body. He grinned at the view of her cleavage as she turned back to smile at him. "You changed, too," she whispered.

"Yeah, there was a lot to choose from in my room."

"In mine, too," Kyle muttered, stepping towards them. He had changed into shorts and a round neck with a matching hat.

"You look good, roommate," Jamie complemented. "Where is Lily?"

"Over here," Lily answered from a corner. Jamie paused as he saw her in a short, form-fitting dress. The dress accentuated her figure more than her previous clothing did. Lily wasn't still wearing a bra. Through the dress, he could make out the tiny dot of her nipples as well as her hips swaying beneath the dress as she walked towards them.

"Uhm, you changed, too," Jamie cleared his throat.

Lily nodded and stared at her feet, obviously aware of his eyes taking in how astonishing she looked. The silence that rose between them would have been awkward if Rebecca didn't suddenly approach all four of them. "Welcome," she greeted. "Now, if everyone could get seated so we could have lunch and talk?"

Jamie looked around the room for the first time. Ron had brought them all to a large dining hall. The walls were tall and wide, giving the feel of a Victorian court. At the middle of the hall sat the dining table, filled with bowls of food – veggies, fruits, steak, soup and bread. Jamie felt his stomach rumble in hunger.

"Come," Rebecca urged, heading for the table. She waited for Ron to pull out a chair for her. Then, she paused and pointed to the rest of the chairs for them to sit.

"Well, a nice hot shower. Then, lunch like kings. I am in," Kyle muttered and headed for the closest chair to Rebecca.

Lily and Peyton followed suit while Jamie stared around the hall one last time. *It isn't a dream, Jamie,* he muttered to himself. He was in a world he probably would never understand.

Rebecca promised them answers, but he suspected that there was more to Cartoonia than anyone could understand in a lifetime.

CHAPTER SIX

Lily sat with her eyes fixated on the walls around them. The dining hall had long walls, long curtains and a dining table made from fine wood. She watched Rebecca and Ron intently, feeling as if someone had to. Somehow, she could feel as if they were in an enemy's den. She couldn't explain if it was Cartoonia warning her, or if that was just her instinct. In the years that she had survived alone without her mother, she had learned to trust no one, especially if they were holding all the cards. Not trusting people was how she had been able to keep the book safe or even stay alive. People hardly helped other people without wanting something in return. If Rebecca was offering them rooms in a twin-mansion she had probably lived in for many years, she wanted something in return. Lily wasn't buying her kindness.

"What about Jer?" Lily asked as Jamie joined them at the table, choosing the chair between Rebecca and Peyton. Jamie looked around, noticing that Jer wasn't with them for the first time.

"Jer is running an errand," Rebecca answered, helping Jamie to be comfortable. She reached for the bowl of grapes on the table, picked out a few onto her plate and passed the bowl to him "He will join us soon."

Ron, noticing that they were all seated and ready to eat, drew out a chair and sat, too.

"So, what is it?" Lily whispered, watching as Jamie also picked a bunch of grapes and passed the bowl to Peyton.

"What is what?" Rebecca raised an eyebrow.

"The relationship between you all three of you. In a twin-mansion on an island as big as this. It almost seems as if…"

"…the island, including Jer and Ron, answer to me?" Rebecca finished with a smile.

That made Peyton pause in between serving herself some of the grapes. Lily noticed that Jamie and Kyle seemed unsettled by Rebecca's unflinching response, too.

"Lily?" Jamie whispered, trying to chide her with his eyes.

"It is fine," Rebecca raised her hand. She turned towards Lily and smiled. "At this point," she said. "You can ask me whatever you want and I will give answers if I have them."

"And I think you have the answer to this particular question, Lily. One of the men seated at this table already belongs to you, yes?"

"Belong?" Lily shook her head.

"Filled with lust for you, if that seems more appropriate," Rebecca iterated. "Probably also makes your body reel with ecstasy with just a glare or a single touch. This man fills your inside with the whole of him, making you complete. I am sure these already happened, or you wouldn't have made it out of Stone Edge, alive."

Lily swallowed. Half of the feeling that Rebecca described was what she had felt with Kyle. The other half? Her eyes briefly steered towards Jamie. Beside him, Peyton finally finished dishing her grapes and began to pass the bowl to her. She deliberately didn't let go of the bowl for a second as Lily instinctively reached over the table to collect it from her. Her eyes burned with a warning Lily couldn't miss.

"You have nothing to say to this, Lily?" Rebecca asked as Lily slid back into her seat.

"Yes," Lily answered, clearing her throat. She straightened her back and tried not to look at anyone as she picked a few grapes from the bowl. "Yes, you are right. They already happened."

"And who is it – Kyle or Jamie?" Rebecca asked.

Lily raised her eyes and suddenly felt nervous. "Kyle," she quickly answered.

"Good," Rebecca smiled. She threw two grapes into her mouth and kept her gaze directed at her. "You should do well to remember that."

Lily felt her defences coming back up. "So, what is it?" she asked again. "You didn't really answer my question."

"Yes, I didn't," Rebecca threw more grapes into her mouth. "Jer and Ron are both my lovers. They answer to me and I, to them."

"So, you are tied together?" Lily whispered.

"Yes, we are," Rebecca's gaze briefly swept towards Ron.

Jamie, who had begun to eat his grapes, cleared his throat and interrupted them. "You mentioned that all three of you aren't originally from Cartoonia," he asked. "You all were brought here at the same time?"

Ron replied his question instead as Rebecca turned to the large plate of steak next after finishing with her grapes. "Yes, with one other." he said.

"One other? There is someone else?" Jamie frowned.

Ron kept quiet and said nothing else, allowing Rebecca to return to answering their questions. "Yes," she nodded. "There was someone else with us, but she isn't here anymore."

Lily shook her head, trying to understand what could have happened to the last member of Rebecca's group. Rebecca and Ron didn't look like they were worried that she wasn't on the island with them. Inching forward in her chair, Lily set her plate aside and wanted to ask more questions. The doors into the dining hall, however, swept open with a loud creak, interrupting the whole conversation. Jer stepped in, nodded at everyone and pulled out a chair beside Kyle. "Apologies for my lateness," he greeted. "I didn't miss much, did I?"

"No, our visitors are just getting started with questions about why we are here." Rebecca kept her eyes on him, almost as if she was expecting something. Jer sat before he shook his head at her. Rebecca didn't look pleased. She gritted her teeth and nearly tore too deep into the steak she was trying to get off the bowl. "Is everything okay?" Lily asked.

The displeasure on Rebecca's face rolled under a forced smile. "No, not at all," she whispered. "You were asking some questions, weren't you?"

Lily wanted to go back to the fourth member of Rebecca's group. But Jamie interrupted again with another question – a crucial question. "What is this place, Rebecca?" he asked. "And why are we in it?"

"Good question, Jamie," Rebecca leaned back in her chair. "You should already guess that this – the whole of Cartoonia – is a world…a universe, unlike the one you – we all came from."

"Yes," Lily heard Jamie, Kyle and Peyton whisper at the same time. To her, Rebecca still wasn't giving direct answers to their questions.

"Cartoonia is magic," Rebecca continued. "Nobody knows what kind of magic it is or where it came from. All anybody knows that it is magic that cannot be broken."

"What do you mean it cannot be broken?" Kyle asked, speaking for the first time since they all sat around the dining table. Apart from grapes, he had poured himself some wine and was now feasting on a piece of steak.

"Once you are in here, you cannot fight Cartoonia's magic or Areeyah's," Rebecca explained. "You only do whatever Cartoonia wants you to do. You know what it wants through firestorm – the beacon that guides the rest of you."

"Fire-storm?" Lily whispered.

"Yeah, and what is Areeyah?" Peyton muttered.

"What is Areeyah?" Rebecca stared at each of their faces, looking surprised. "There is so much you ought to have known," she shook her head.

"The book," she continued. "It was it that brought you here, wasn't it?" she asked.

Lily nodded. "It brings everyone here."

"Yes, it does. But then, it also chooses its holder. It chooses its firestorm."

Rebecca stopped talking to stare directly at her. Lily watched as everyone stopped eating and turned to her as well. "Areeyah is the book," Kyle spoke first. "And you are the firestorm," Peyton grunted.

"Yes, she is," Rebecca smiled. "Areeyah tells her everything she needs to know. Everything you all need to know, so Cartoonia gets what it wants."

"And what does it want?" Lily muttered, afraid the answer wouldn't be what she, Jamie, Kyle or Peyton would want to hear.

"It wants lust always," Rebecca whispered. "It wants eternity. It wants to be here forever, and there is nothing we can all do to fight that."

"Hold on. Hold on," Jamie suddenly shoved his plate aside. "I am not sure I completely understand. So, there is Cartoonia, this, uhm, alternative world that has a magic no one can resist. Then, there is Areeyah, the book that brings humans into Cartoonia. This book chooses who it shares Cartoonia's secrets with. We also have the firestorm, which happens to be Lily?"

"There isn't just one firestorm," Jer spoke. "For each group or person that makes it into Cartoonia, Areeyah chooses who to use as its eyes, mind and ears."

"Eyes, mind and ears?"

"Yeah, much like a spokesperson. Someone that lets the others know what is required for survival."

"Who was your firestorm?" Lily suddenly asked.

The table fell quiet. Rebecca stared at Jer and Ron and shook her head. Ron seemed utterly obedient to her, but Jer cleared his throat and responded to her question. "Her name was Rachel," he said. "Areeyah brought us all here while we were gathered in a museum in New York."

"Was she the one that opened the book – your firestorm?" Kyle asked.

"Yes."

"Well, so refreshing to know Lily isn't the first to do something stupid that gets people where they do not want to go," Peyton remarked, raising her eyebrows at her.

Lily ignored her and turned to Jer. "When did this happen? How long have you all been here?"

Jer parted his lips to speak, but Rebecca flew back into the conversation. "It doesn't matter how long," she gritted her teeth.

"Twenty years," Jer said in an almost inaudible whisper.

Lily wasn't sure she had heard him correctly. "I am sorry?"

"Twenty years," Jer repeated. "Seven thousand, two hundred and ninety-eight days to be precise."

Jamie, Kyle and Peyton's faces drained of colour. "Wha—what?" Peyton stuttered.

"You have all been here for two decades?" Kyle's eyes widened at them and then at the high walls around them.

Jer turned to Rebecca. "Tell them, Rebecca," he said. "Tell them no one ever comes here and gets to leave. Tell them the only way anyone leaves is if they choose the only option Cartoonia gives – betray the others and find the exit port."

EPILOGUE

Alpha was the first to hold her legs apart and bury his big cock inside her. Rachel gritted her teeth as pleasure she had never felt before swept through every inch of her body. Her eyes darted uncontrollably in their sockets while her toes and fingers tingled with pleasure. She wrapped her legs around him, getting him to shove in deeper, with more pleasure almost stopping her heart.

Once Alpha was fully inside her, the rest of the pack closed in around her. One of them held his cock above her lips, waited until she opened her mouth, and then filled her throat with his cock. The other two ran their hands over the rest of her body, caressing her breasts, her abdomen and her naked thighs. They touched her everywhere, waking deep-seated lust and driving her nuts with overwhelming pleasure.

Alpha was swift and steady with his thrust. And so was the member of his pack that filled her mouth with his cock. Both of them moved rhythmically, dashing in and out of her, and making her groan for more. Filled with a lust she couldn't explain, she gripped the cock of the third man, squeezed hard and began to jerk his rigid meat. He paused and let her get comfortable with touching him before he gripped one of her breasts and slowly started to dance to the movement of her palm. He grunted, urging her to squeeze him harder and watch as the muscles on his body rippled with his growing pleasure.

Soon, she let go of him as the entire room echoed with male grunts, coupled with her moan. Alpha, having had enough of pummeling inside her squirming cunt, withdrew eventually, allowing the last member of his pack to take over. He stepped away and watched with a smile over his face.

Although Rachel could hardly speak with his pack feasting on her body like a morning snack, she watched him intently, getting closer to her climax just by watching his hard cock between his legs.

"You would have what you want soon, Rachel," she heard him say from where he stood. "You will go back home, free, but haunted by what you have done."

Haunted. It was so little, compared to what she had imagined would happen once she returned home.

Alpha smiled as if he could read her mind. "You will never find your way back here, no matter how you try," he said. "But someone else will. Someone always does."

"And your fate will be theirs."

Rachel closed her eyes, feeling her release finally taking over every inch of her body.